A Pokén

#8

Pokémon
junior

There are more books about Pokémon for younger readers.

COLLECT THEM ALL!

COMING SOON!

A Pokémon Snow-down

Pokémon junior

#8

Adapted by S. E. Heller

SCHOLASTIC INC.
New York Toronto London Auckland Sydney
Mexico City New Delhi Hong Kong

ISBN 0-439-20097-0

12   8 9/0

Printed in the U.S.A.

First Scholastic printing, January 2001

A Pokémon Snow-down

Pokémon
junior

#8

CHAPTER ONE

Ash Takes the Lead

Pikachu was happy. It was on another adventure with its trainer, Ash. Ash's friends Misty and Brock were there, too. Ash was on a mission to become the world's greatest Pokémon trainer. Misty, Brock, and Pikachu were helping him.

"*Pika?*" the little yellow Pokémon

1

asked. They had come to a fork in the road. Which way should they go?

"That way!" Ash said.

"No, Ash," Brock said. "That trail leads up a mountain."

"I do not want to climb a mountain!" Misty cried.

"It is just a little hill," said Ash. "Come on, Pikachu!"

Pikachu was excited to explore the mountain. Misty and Brock followed. But

they were nervous.

"I hope you know what you are doing," Misty told Ash.

Soon the mountain became steep and snowy.

"This is *not* a little hill," Misty said. "It's a huge mountain!"

"I think we should turn around," said Brock.

"A Pokémon Master does not give up," said Ash. "A little snow will not stop me!"

"*Pika!*" agreed Pikachu.

The friends climbed and climbed. It was snowing harder and harder.

"I am freezing!" Misty said. "How much farther is it to the top?"

Brock checked his compass. It was supposed to point north. But it was not. It was going crazy!

"What does that mean?" cried Misty.

"We are lost," Brock said.

Misty was mad at Ash. She shivered. It was freezing!

"Ash, you made us climb this mountain. Now we are stuck. And

4

it is up to you to get us off!" Misty yelled.

Pikachu was worried. It looked at Ash. What would they do now?

Ash was thinking. Then he had an idea.

"Pidgeotto, I choose you!" he cried.

Ash held a Poké Ball high. Out came Pidgeotto, flapping its wings.

"Find a path down the mountain," Ash told Pidgeotto.

The Flying Pokémon went high. It could see a trail.

"Good job, Pidgeotto!" said Ash.
Pikachu smiled. Soon everything
would be okay!

CHAPTER TWO

Snow Rolls for Jessie

"Why did they have to go the snowy way?" Meowth moaned.

Meowth was part of Team Rocket, Ash's and Pikachu's enemies. Team Rocket was teenagers Jessie and James. They were always trying to steal Pikachu for their boss.

But today Meowth
did not want to
chase Pikachu. It
was too cold on this
mountain. Meowth
wanted to go someplace warm.

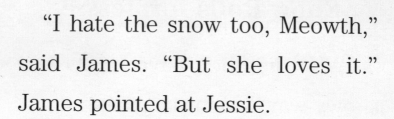

"I hate the snow too, Meowth,"
said James. "But she loves it."
James pointed at Jessie.

"Snow, snow, I love it so," sang
Jessie. She was very happy.

"The snow is making her a little
flaky," Meowth told James.

"Mother used to make food out
of snow," Jessie told her friends.

"Snow rolls were the best, with just a little soy sauce!"

"That sounds awful!" said James.

Yuck! thought Meowth. It wanted some nice, hot food.

"We should go get them," James said. "We can use the balloon."

Jessie and James looked at each other. They smiled. They had a plan!

"To protect the world from devastation," Jessie said.

"To unite all people within our nation," said James.

9

"To denounce —" Jessie began.

"Wait, stop!" Meowth yelled.
"The balloon is floating away!"

They all ran after the balloon.
But they were too late.

"Wait, come back!" Jessie yelled.

"We need the hot air!" Meowth
shouted.

The balloon was gone.
Now they were stuck
on the mountain. And it
was starting to snow!
"What will we do?"
cried James.
"What will

we eat?" asked Meowth.

With a happy smile, Jessie turned to her friends. "I can make snow rolls!" she told them. Then she frowned. "If only the soy sauce was not on the balloon!"

CHAPTER THREE

Pikachu Blows Away

Meanwhile, the wind and snow made it hard for Pikachu, Ash, and their friends to see. It was getting dark and stormy.

"We should dig a snow cave for the night," said Brock.

Ash wanted to keep going. "The trail *has* to be close! We will find it

soon," he said. "We have to!"

"Even the bravest Pokémon Master would stop," said Brock. "This is a bad snowstorm. It will be even worse after dark."

"Okay," said Ash. He knew Brock was right.

But as the friends got ready to dig, a gust of wind knocked them down.

"*Pika!*" cried Pikachu. The Electric Mouse Pokémon went flying in the wind. It could not stop.

"Pikachu!" cried Ash. He started to run after his Pokémon.

"Ash, stay here! You will get lost out there," Brock called.

But Ash did not listen. He ran after Pikachu. The snow was deep and thick. He could not keep up. And soon Brock and Misty could not see him anymore.

The wind swept Pikachu over a cliff. "*Pika, pika!*" cried the little yellow Pokémon.

Pikachu grabbed onto a rock as it fell. "*Pikachuuuu!*" it cried.

"Pikachu, where are you?" called Ash.

CHAPTER FOUR

Bulbasaur to the Rescue

Pikachu was scared. It would not be able to hold on for long. And it could not see Ash.

"*Pikachuuu!*" it cried. There was no answer. Pikachu cried again and again. Finally, it could hear Ash.

"I am here, Pikachu!" Ash called

out. "Grab my hand!"

The little Pokémon stretched its arm as far as it could. Ash stretched, too. They were so close!

"*Pikachuuu!*"

Oh, no! Pikachu lost its grip on the rock. It was falling!

The little Pokémon grabbed onto another rock. It would never be able to reach Ash now. What would happen?

"Bulbasaur, I choose you!" called Ash.

The Plant Pokémon saw Pikachu far below. Bulbasaur wanted to help its friend.

"Bulbasaur, use your Vine Whip to pull up Pikachu!" said Ash.

Bulbasaur lowered a vine from the plant on its back.

"Hold on tight, Pikachu! We will pull you up!" yelled Ash.

Pikachu tried to grab the vine, but it slipped. It was falling! Pikachu screamed. So did Ash!

But Bulbasaur knew what to do. It threw more vines over the cliff. The long vines wrapped around

Pikachu and caught it. The little Pokémon was safe!

"*Bulbasaur!*" said the Plant Pokémon. It was glad Pikachu was okay.

"Nice job!" said Ash. He was proud of Bulbasaur. Leaning over, Ash pulled on the vines. Soon, Pikachu was on top of the cliff again.

"*Pika pi!*" cried Pikachu as it hugged Ash. They were so

happy to be together, they almost started to cry.

"I thought I had lost you," Ash told Pikachu.

"*Pikachu*," said the Pokémon. *Me, too.* Pikachu had thought it would never see Ash again.

"*Bulba*," said Bulbasaur. Even the hero had been scared!

CHAPTER FIVE

Snowed In

"Pikachu?" What do we do now?

Pikachu was worried. They needed to find Misty and Brock. It was getting dark fast.

Ash tried to climb back up the slope, but it was too steep.

"Misty! Brock!" yelled Ash. The

wind was howling. It was so noisy, Misty and Brock could not hear them.

"*Pika!*" said Pikachu. They had to spend the night here.

"We can dig a snow cave," said Ash. He tried to dig with his hands, but the snow was so cold it hurt.

"I have an idea," said Ash. "Charmander can help." He pulled out a Poké Ball. "Charmander, I choose you!"

Charmander appeared in a flash.

Pikachu was happy to see the Fire Pokémon.

"Charmander! Use your Flamethrower to melt the snow!" said Ash.

Charmander opened its mouth. Fire shot out. It melted a big hole in the icy wall.

"Not bad!" said Ash with a smile. That hole would make a great snow cave.

Next Ash called Bulbasaur and Squirtle.

"*Bulbasaur!*" cried the Plant Pokémon.

"*Squirtle!*" cried the Tiny Turtle Pokémon.

The Pokémon were ready to help.

The friends all climbed inside the cave. Together they piled up snow. Soon they closed off the cave.

Now no wind could get in. But it was still cold. Ash and his Pokémon shivered.

"Okay, everyone. Let's get around Charmander's flame," said Ash.

Charmander held up its tail. At

the end was a little flame. Charmander made the fire bigger and hotter.

"*Pika!*" cried Pikachu. *That feels good.*

"*Bulba!*" cried Bulbasaur. *Yes!*

"*Squirtle!*" said Squirtle. *Aaah!*

Charmander's friends were happy.

"The heat is on!" said Ash happily. Maybe this night would not be so cold after all.

CHAPTER SIX

Meowth's Hot Idea

"We are doomed!" cried James. He was inside an igloo Team Rocket had built. His teeth were chattering.

"This candle is our last bit of heat!" cried Meowth.

Just then, the flame blew out. Meowth looked for another match

to light the candle. But there were all used up.

"We could pretend they are heating lamps," said Meowth. "Maybe if we *think* warm we will *feel* warm."

Jessie, James, and Meowth each took a match. They closed their eyes.

"I am in a hot spring," Meowth imagined. "The water is so warm."

"This sunny beach is perfect!" dreamed James.

Jessie pretended to be in a hot

desert. "I wish I had a fan!"

Meowth and James were so happy in their daydreams, they fell asleep. But Jessie did not. She opened her eyes.

"Wake up! Wake up!" she cried when she saw her friends sleeping. Jessie knew it was not good to fall asleep in the cold. They would freeze!

James and Meowth did not want to wake up. But Jessie made them.

Team Rocket would have to help one another stay awake.

Jessie pinched Meowth's and James's cheeks.

"Ouch!" said James.

"Ouch!" cried Meowth.

But no matter how much it hurt, they had to stay awake.

CHAPTER SEVEN

The Warmth of Friendship

Charmander did not look good. The Fire Pokémon was tired. It was sweating hard.

"What is wrong?" Ash asked.

"*Char*," said Charmander weakly. Its flame was almost all used up.

Ash was worried.

"Go back in your Poké Ball and

rest," said Ash. He looked at the others. "All of you, return. It will be warmer for you in your Poké Balls."

But the Pokémon did not want to leave Ash alone in the cold.

"*Char!*" cried Charmander. *No!*

"*Squirtle!*" cried Squirtle in protest.

"*Bulbasaur!*" Bulbasaur did not want to go to into its Poké Ball, either.

But Ash made them all go in. Then he turned to Pikachu.

"You too, Pikachu," said Ash. "I

31

want you to be warm."

"*Pika pika pi!*" said Pikachu.
I am staying with you!
The little yellow
Pokémon ran to its
friend, hugging him.

"Oh, Pikachu!" cried
Ash. "You want to stay
out to keep me warm?"

"*Pika,*" Pikachu said, nodding.

Ash held Pikachu tight. It was
very cold. Ash was shivering, but
he was still worried about his
Pokémon.

"I hope they will be warm

enough," he said. He took off his vest and folded the Poké Balls inside it. He was even colder than before, but he did not care. He wrapped the vest around Pikachu.

Suddenly, a blast of wind broke a hole in the cave! The icy air was freezing.

"Ahhh!" cried Ash. He ran to the hole and sat against it to block the wind. His teeth chattered with the cold.

"*Pika!*" cried Pikachu. *No!* If Ash sat there all night, he would freeze!

"Go into your Poké Ball!" Ash ordered Pikachu. "I will be okay if I know you are safe."

"*Pikachu!*" The little Pokémon would not leave Ash! It hugged Ash harder, trying to warm him up.

Just then, all of the Pokémon came out of their Poké Balls. They could not stand to see their trainer suffer.

"Squirtle!"

"Bulbasaur!"

"Char!"

"Pidgeotto!"

Pidgeotto wrapped its wings around Ash. The others hugged him tight.

"My friends," said Ash with a smile. He was overcome by their love. "I guess we will all be cold together."

"Pika," said Pikachu. They would get through the night together.

CHAPTER EIGHT

Rescued!

The next morning was sunny and bright. Ash and his Pokémon walked out of their cave and stretched. Pikachu smiled at its friends. The cold night was over at last!

"Ash!" cried Brock and Misty.

Pikachu looked up to see its

human friends above them on the cliff.

"I am so glad to see you!" cried Ash.

"*Pika!*" said Pikachu. *Me, too!*

Pikachu and Ash were also happy to see Brock's Rock Pokémon, Onix. Onix looked like a giant stone snake. It picked them up on its back and carried them to the top of the cliff.

"You will never guess where we spent the night," said Misty. "Onix dug a tunnel right into a

hot spring! It was so warm!"

"And look what floated in!" said Brock. It was Team Rocket's hot air balloon.

"Finder's keepers," Misty laughed.

Brock called Vulpix. The Fire Pokémon used its Flame-thrower Attack to heat up the air in the balloon. Soon the friends were floating away from the mountain.

"Do you hear something?" Ash asked.

Misty and Brock shook their heads. They did not know that Team Rocket was running below them.

"Wait! That is our balloon!" cried Jessie.

"Stop!" yelled James and Meowth.

Team Rocket did not watch where they were going. *Splash!* Team Rocket fell right into the hot spring!

"Ahh!" cried Jessie.

"Meowth's dream came true!" said James.

"It is so warm!" said Meowth.

Overhead, the hot air balloon floated by. Pikachu was happy to see a town ahead. It was ready for a new adventure. Hopefully, it would be a warm one!

Snorlax Strikes Back!

Pokémon junior

Chapter Book #9:
Snorlax Takes a Stand

Snorlax is one of Ash's most stubborn Pokémon. All it does is sleep! Then Team Rocket tries to steal food from all the Pokémon on the Orange Islands. Only Snorlax can stop them. But can Ash wake up the portly Pokémon in time?

Coming soon to a bookstore near you!
Visit us at www.scholastic.com

SCHOLASTIC

POKJR999